The SECRET RIVER

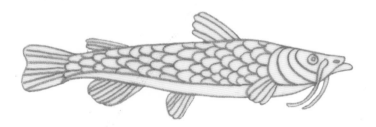

The SECRET RIVER

MARJORIE KINNAN RAWLINGS

&

LEONARD WEISGARD

ATHENEUM BOOKS FOR YOUNG READERS
New York London Toronto Sydney

 here is a dark forest far away in Florida. The trees are so tall that the sky is like a blue veil over their leafy hair.

There is a path through the forest. It leads to the home of Calpurnia and Buggy-horse.

Calpurnia is a little girl and Buggy-horse is her dog. Her name is Calpurnia because she was born to be a poet. Buggy-horse is a peculiar name, but even when he was a puppy, his back dipped in the middle and he had an enormously fat stomach, just like a little old buggy horse. He could not possibly have been called Rex or Rover or any ordinary name for a dog. Calpurnia wrote her first poem about him:

> *My dog's name is Buggy-horse.*
> *Of course.*

On the morning when this story begins, Calpurnia was awakened very early. Outside her window, two red-birds were singing to each other. They sang so loud that she heard them in her sleep, and she woke up. She listened, and she decided that one red-bird was singing "Love me? Love me? Love me?" and the other red-bird was singing "Sure do. Sure do. Sure do." Calpurnia looked over the side of her bed. Buggy-horse was still sound asleep.

She said to him, "Wake up, my dear dog. I have a feeling something special is going to happen today."

Buggy-horse just stretched himself and yawned. He was a lazy dog. He liked to sleep for hours and hours, sometimes in the sunshine and sometimes in the shade. He hoped Calpurnia was not getting ready for an adventure. He was obliged to follow her wherever she went, because he was miserable when she was out of sight.

Calpurnia washed her face and hands and brushed her teeth and combed her hair. Because of her feeling, she put on her best pink hair ribbons. She made her bed neatly.

She went out-of-doors with Buggy-horse and saw that it was indeed a beautiful day. The sun was shining and the oranges on the trees were as bright as balls of gold. She said a poem:

> Lovely day,
>   come what may.
>   If I did not love
>   my mother
>   and my father
>   I would run away.
>   Because
>   it is a running-away
>   kind of day.

As it turned out, she had the best reason in the world for making a journey.

Her mother called, "You two little hungry things, come and get your breakfast."

At breakfast Calpurnia's father said, "Hard times have come to the forest."

She said, "What are hard times?"

"It means that everything is hard, and especially for poor people."

She felt the table, she laid her hand on Buggy-horse's hard back, and it was true: Everything seemed harder than usual.

She asked, "Are we poor people? I don't feel poor."

Her father said, "We are poor people. I make an honest living selling fish to other poor people. Now there are no fish. Nobody can catch any fish. I shall have to close my fish market, and things will go hard with all of us."

Calpurnia ate her hard grits and patted Buggy-horse's back and she said a poem:

I wish
we had fish.
Then hard times would end.
But I am not the least bit worried,
　　　because
everybody be's my friend.

Her mother said, "You can't say 'everybody be's my friend.' It sounds as if you're talking about bees. Honeybees or bumblebees."

Calpurnia was delighted. She changed her poem in her mind and then she said:

Everybody's bees is my friends.
Everybody's flowers is my flowers.
Everybody's happy hours
　　　is my happy hours.
All this goes on
　　　and there is no ends.

"That's better," said her mother. "You are really a smart child. But you should say 'are no ends.'"

So Calpurnia said, "Are no ends. Are, are, are," and Buggy-horse said, "Arf, arf, arf."

Her mother said, "I sometimes don't know who's smartest, you or that little old Buggy-horse dog."

Her father said, "It won't matter who's the smartest if I can't get fish to sell to the other poor people," and he went to his empty fish market.

Calpurnia went outside and stood beside a tree and thought about the fish market. There was a small pond where she and Buggy-horse often went to fish, but she had never caught anything there except tiny minnows. Also, she used angleworms for bait, and they were squirmy and had to be kept in a glass jar. She did not like this and she imagined that the angleworms did not like it either.

She said to herself, "Now if I was a fish, what would I like to bite?"

She thought and thought, and she had a wonderful idea.

She said to Buggy-horse, "If I was a fish, I would only bite something unusual and something pretty."

She remembered some beautiful pink crepe paper, left over from a birthday party.

"Mother dear, may I make some pink paper roses?"

"Of course, my child." Her mother was very considerate and did not ask questions unless she had to. So Calpurnia made some large roses from the pink paper and tied them to her pigtails. She set out with Buggy-horse and her fishing pole to find Mother Albirtha, who was the wisest person in the forest. Mother Albirtha was sitting in front of her little shop. She was worried about hard times too, like Calpurnia's father, for if there are no fish, and one person is poor, then everybody else is poor too, and Mother Albirtha had no customers at all.

Calpurnia said, "Mother Albirtha, I am going fishing, to keep my father from being poor. I have fished in the pond, but the fish there are so small. You are the wisest person in the forest. Will you tell me where I can catch some big fish, so that hard times will be soft times?"

Mother Albirtha rocked back and forth.

She said, "Child, I have not breathed this to a living soul, but I will tell you. There are big fish in the secret river. Oh my, the fish! Catfish, perch, bream, mudfish, and garfish. Especially catfish."

"Is the secret river far away?"

"Nobody knows."

"How will I find it?"

"You will know the river when you see it. Just follow your nose."

"Thank you, Mother Albirtha. When I catch the fish, I will bring you some."

"Child, you talk like an angel."

Now Calpurnia thought it was foolish to find anything by following her nose.

She said to Buggy-horse, "My nose goes straight ahead. How will I know where to turn?"

But she started out into the forest. The first thing she knew, a rabbit hopped by. She turned to look at him, which meant that her nose pointed to the right. So she followed her nose. After a while, a blue jay flew into a live-oak tree. She turned her nose to the left, to look at him. So she followed her nose. All of a sudden she heard a sound like music. The forest had ended. And in front of her was a river—a river she had never seen before. Calpurnia had found the secret river. The river was so beautiful that she sat down on a cypress knee to admire it.

She said to the cypress trees, "I hope you don't mind if I sit on one of your knees to admire the secret river."

The cypresses clicked their green needles, which she took for permission. The river was singing as it ran by. Then she saw the fish. They were jumping and dancing, and there were so many of them that they got in each other's way.

Calpurnia said to the fish, "Do you mind if I catch some of you, to save the forest from hard times?"

The fish did not answer, so she took that for permission, too. Now she saw a little red boat tied to the bank. It had a sign on it. The sign said:

PLEASE TIE ME UP AGAIN WHEN YOU ARE THROUGH WITH ME. I AM SO AFRAID OF GETTING LOST.

Calpurnia stepped into the red boat with her fishing pole and the pink paper roses tied to her pigtails. Buggy-horse followed her into the boat. She pushed away from the shore. Then she took one of the pink paper roses from her braids and tied it to the hook on the end of her fishing line. The pink rose floated for a few minutes, and then sank slowly down through the water. An old frog sitting on the bottom of the river saw it.

He croaked, "Now what in the water is that thing? It's meant to catch fish, that's what it is. Well, I won't bite it, that's sure."

He settled himself to watch, and before he had blinked his eyes, a huge catfish tried to swallow the pink paper rose, and was hauled out of the river on the end of Calpurnia's fishing line.

The old frog grunted. "I knew it. There is nothing more foolish than a fish."

Sitting in the red boat, Calpurnia pulled in one fish after another. Buggy-horse hung over the side in excitement. Just as Mother Albirtha had promised, there were more catfish than anything else, and this pleased Calpurnia for two reasons. In the first place, the people in the forest dearly loved to eat catfish, and her father could get a higher price for them. In the second place, catfish are extremely disagreeable and try to stick everybody with the sharp barbs on their heads. Calpurnia thought that fish who go out of their way to stick people deserve to be caught.

After a while, Calpurnia had as many catfish in the red boat as she could possibly carry home. She pushed the boat into the shore and tied it carefully to the trunk of a cypress tree. She moved the fish to the ground, and Buggy-horse helped her. He could only carry one fish in his mouth at a time, but he worked hard and did his best.

Calpurnia said to him, "How can we carry all these fish home?"

Buggy-horse looked at the fishing pole and barked. He looked at a clump of bear grass and barked. Calpurnia understood at once. Bear grass has long, thin, tough leaves, and they can be used like strong pieces of string. She broke off the leaves and passed them through the gills of the fish, and tied the fish onto the fishing pole. She put the pole over her shoulder. It was very heavy with all the catfish on it. She started out for home.

Calpurnia said to Buggy-horse, "Mother Albirtha told us to find the secret river by following my nose. Do you think we can get home the same way?"

Buggy-horse barked, and she decided to try and get home the same way. A gray fox turned her nose to the left, and a mother raccoon with two baby raccoons turned her nose to the right. It was getting dark. The sun had set; the night animals were coming out to play and hunt for their supper. Calpurnia heard a strange sound.

A deep voice called, "Who-o-o-o? Why-y-y-y? Who?"

Calpurnia did not know where the questions came from, but she answered bravely, "I'm Calpurnia. Who are you?"

The voice said, "Who-o-o-o."

"Why, it's just a hoot-owl."

But then she saw the hoot-owl sitting in the top of a dead tree. He was enormous, and he did not look friendly. She wondered if he had come out to hunt for his supper. He rolled his big round eyes at her fish. He rolled his big round eyes at Buggy-horse. No doubt about it—he was very hungry.

Calpurnia said quickly, "Please, Mister Hoot-owl, can I give you a nice fresh catfish for your supper?"

The hoot-owl cocked his head on one side and flapped his wings. He flew down into a small wild plum tree beside her. It was a great deal of trouble to untie the catfish from the fishing pole, but she picked out the biggest fish of all and laid it on the clean grass. The hoot-owl swooped down and began eating it at once, without saying "thank you."

Calpurnia said, "You are welcome anyway."

The forest was so dark, she could not see her nose in front of her face, so of course she could not follow her nose.

"I'm not a bit worried," she said out loud. She *was* really worried, but she said it to cheer up Buggy-horse.

All of a sudden she saw a huge black shadow in front
of her. The shadow moved and Buggy-horse growled.

The shadow was a big black bear. Calpurnia's heart
went *thump-thump-thump*. Buggy-horse tried to hide
behind the catfish.

Calpurnia thought, *Maybe the bear is hungry too.*

"Mister Bear, could I interest you in a nice fresh catfish
for your supper?" she asked.

The bear snuffled, as if he needed a handkerchief,
and he came closer. She did not wait to pick out the
biggest catfish. She pulled two from the fishing pole as
fast as possible and laid them on the grass. She did not
run away, but she hurried. She called over her shoulder,
"You're entirely welcome," in case the bear had
thanked her.

Then Calpurnia saw something crouching ahead of her. It was a panther. She did not know whether he was friendly or unfriendly, but she thought, *I'm sure he's hungry. I expect hard times have even come to the panthers in the forest.*

So she said, "Mister Panther, you are sort of a cat, and cats love fish, and I should like to give you some nice fresh catfish for your supper."

She was not so frightened now, and she took three catfish from her fishing pole and laid them on the clean grass.

The panther began eating them at once, and he purred so loudly that she knew he was saying "thank you."

She said, "You are certainly most welcome."

She said a poem:

> *If somebody scares you, the thing to do*
> *is give somebody something to do.*
> *Then they never bother you.*
> *Sometimes they say "thank you."*

Calpurnia and Buggy-horse went on. And then the
full moon rose and the forest was as bright as day. She
smelled night flowers blooming.

A white crane flew straight across the moon. It
dropped a white feather, and Calpurnia picked it up and
tucked it in her hair.

And then she saw that they were out of the forest and
on the path home. Buggy-horse barked joyfully and ran
ahead.

Calpurnia said, "It would be nice to go home this
minute, but I promised Mother Albirtha some fish. So
come, my dear dog."

Mother Albirtha was just turning off the light in her shop when she heard the knock on her door.

"Who is that, knocking so late?" she called.

"It is Calpurnia, with your fish."

Mother Albirtha's eyes were as big as saucers when she saw the fish.

"Child, where did you catch all those catfish?"

"Why, in the secret river, where you told me to go."

"Oh my goodness to the may-haw bush. Oh my goodness to the swamp maple."

"How many catfish do you want, Mother Albirtha?" Calpurnia asked.

"Oh my goodness to the red-bud tree. Just give me one catfish, child. Just one nice fat catfish."

Calpurnia chose the nicest and fattest and Mother Albirtha wrapped it in her apron. They all said, "Good night," and Calpurnia and Buggy-horse hurried on home.

All the lamps were burning in the house. Calpurnia's mother and father put their arms around her and began to cry.

"Dear daughter, we thought you were lost in the forest."

"Oh, no. I just followed my nose. And see, I brought fish to turn hard times to soft times. I gave some away, but it was necessary."

Her mother and father could not believe their eyes when they saw the catfish.

"Child, how did you catch all these fish? How did you carry them home by yourself? Where have you been?"

But Calpurnia was so tired and so sleepy that she could not answer. She did not know another thing until it was morning. Her father had gone to his market to sell the catfish.

A man who had not had anything to eat for a long time bought the first catfish. He said he would pay for it as soon as he had eaten it and earned money for a day's work, for he had been too weak from hunger to work. A woman who had not had anything to eat for a long time bought the second catfish, and said she would pay for it as soon as she had eaten it and earned money for a day's work, for she had been too weak from hunger to work. All the people from the forest bought catfish and ate them and felt strong again and went out into the world and found work to do. They earned money, and that night they all paid Calpurnia's father for the catfish, and had money to spare. Mother Albirtha had six customers in her shop. And so hard times in the forest turned to soft times.

One day Calpurnia and Buggy-horse started out to find the secret river again. They searched all that day, and all the next day, and the next. Calpurnia followed her nose this way and that way. She found strange flowers and strange birds and strange little pools of water. But she could not find the river. So she went to Mother Albirtha.

"Mother Albirtha," she said, "I cannot find the secret river."

"Child," she said, "this is a sad thing to tell you. There is not any secret river."

"But Mother Albirtha, you told me how to find it, and I found it. I want to find it again."

Mother Albirtha rocked back and forth.

She said, "Child, sometimes a thing happens once, and does not ever happen anymore."

Calpurnia said, "But I want to catch more catfish in the river."

Mother Albirtha said, "Child, you caught catfish when catfish were needed. Hard times have turned to soft times. So you will not find the river again."

"But I saw it. It must be somewhere."

Mother Albirtha rocked back and forth.

'The secret river is in your mind," she said. "You can go there any time you want to. In your mind. Close your eyes, and you will see it."

Calpurnia was delighted. She skipped all the way home. Buggy-horse chased his peculiar tail.

Calpurnia sat down under a magnolia tree and closed her eyes.

She saw the river. It was as beautiful as she remembered it. She made a poem:

The secret river is in my mind.
I can go there anytime.
Everything Mother Albirtha says is true.
The sky is gold and the river is blue.
River, river, I love you.

Marjorie Kinnan Rawlings (August 8, 1896–December 14, 1953) has touched generations of readers with her novel *The Yearling*, which was awarded the Pulitzer Prize in 1939. Reading this novel has become a rite of passage for many, and its fame has earned Marjorie Kinnan Rawlings a place among America's most celebrated authors. Often considered to be a young adult novel, *The Yearling* was in fact not written with that intention in mind. *The Secret River* is the only story Marjorie Rawlings wrote specifically for children.

Marjorie Kinnan Rawlings lived most of her life in Florida and is well known for her ability to capture life in the American South, where most of her writings take place. She is celebrated as a chronicler of the realities of rural life, with a keen understanding of adolescence and growing up.

The Secret River was first published in a slightly longer form posthumously, and was awarded a Newbery Honor in 1956.

To Caitlyn & Lauren: *many thanks.*
And thanks to our great model, Lerato.
—*L. D.* & *D. D.*

ATHENEUM BOOKS FOR YOUNG READERS

An imprint of Simon & Schuster Children's Publishing Division

1230 Avenue of the Americas, New York, New York 10020

Text copyright © 1955 by Charles Scribner's Sons

Text copyright renewed © 1983 by John Sundeman,

Trustee of the Norton Baskin Literary Trust

Illustrations copyright © 2011 by Leo and Diane Dillon

ATHENEUM BOOKS FOR YOUNG READERS is a registered trademark of Simon & Schuster, Inc.

For information about special discounts for bulk purchases,

please contact Simon & Schuster Special Sales

at 1-866-506-1949 or business@simonandschuster.com.

The Simon & Schuster Speakers Bureau can bring authors to your live event.

For more information or to book an event,

contact the Simon & Schuster Speakers Bureau

at 1-866-248-3049 or visit our website at www.simonspeakers.com.

Book design by Leo and Diane Dillon and Lauren Rille

The text for this book is set in Melior.

The illustrations for this book are rendered in acrylic on bristol board.

Manufactured in China

First Edition

1010 SCP

2 4 6 8 10 9 7 5 3 1

Library of Congress Cataloging-in-Publication Data

Rawlings, Marjorie Kinnan, 1896–1953.

The secret river / Marjorie Kinnan Rawlings ; illustrated by Leo and Diane Dillon. — 1st ed.

p. cm.

Summary: Young Calpurnia takes her dog, Buggy-horse,

and follows her nose to a secret river in a Florida forest,

where she catches enough fresh fish to feed her hungry neighbors,

even after giving some to the forest creatures

she meets on the way home.

ISBN 978-1-4169-1179-1

[1. Fishing—Fiction. 2. Hunger—Fiction. 3. Forests and forestry—Fiction.

4. Dogs—Fiction. 5. Forest animals—Fiction. 6. Florida—Fiction.]

I. Dillon, Leo. II. Dillon, Diane. III. Title.

PZ7.R196Se 2011

[Fic]—dc22

2007033292